Doggie Day

Adapted by MacKenzie Buckley

Based on the teleplay "Doggie Day" by Jorge Aguirre

Illustrated by Marilena Perilli and Kuni Tomita

A GOLDEN BOOK • NEW YORK

randomhouse.com/kids

ISBN 978-0-385-37501-6

Printed in the United States of America

10 9 8 7 6 5 4 3 2 1

It was a beautiful morning in Playa Verde, the big city where Dora lived. Dora and her friends were volunteering at the animal shelter.

"I'm so excited for Doggie Adoption Day, Alana!" said Dora.

"Me too," Alana agreed. "So many doggies need homes."

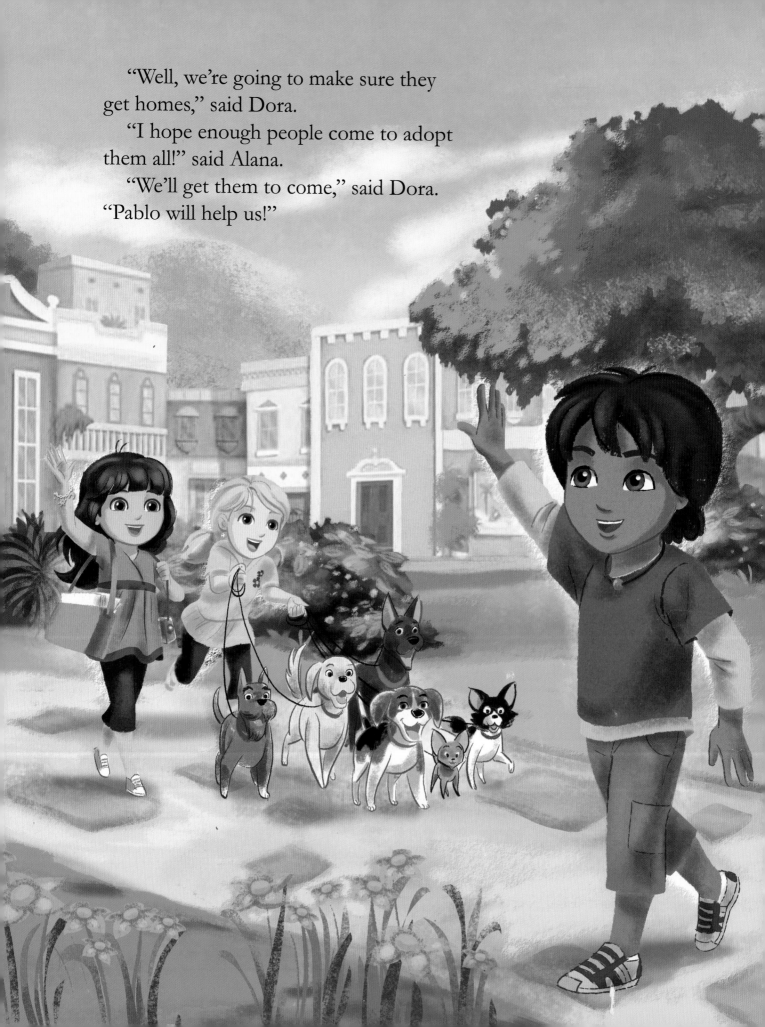

"Well, we're going to make sure they get homes," said Dora.

"I hope enough people come to adopt them all!" said Alana.

"We'll get them to come," said Dora. "Pablo will help us!"

"I will?" asked Pablo nervously as the friendly puppies jumped all over him. "I'm not a dog person. They're just too . . . doggy."

Dora laughed. "Oh, this is perfect for our Doggie Adoption Day video!" She reached into her bag for her camera.

But before Dora
could record the funny
scene, Cusco the beagle
puppy grabbed her
camera in his mouth and ran off.

"¡*Ay, no!*" cried Alana. "Where is Cusco
going? He has to come back so we can find
him a home!"

"Don't worry," Dora told her friend. "Pablo and I will find
Cusco and be back before Doggie Adoption Day starts."

"*Siéntate, perrito.* Sit," Dora said when she and Pablo finally caught up to Cusco.

"Ewww!" Pablo said. "Dora, your camera is covered in dog slobber. You'd better check to see if it still works."

When Dora turned on the camera and pointed it at
Cusco, something amazing happened. Cusco opened
his mouth. But instead of barking, he started to sing!
"My three little brothers are on their own.
Help me find them so we can all have homes!"

"Whoa, Dora—your camera is magic!" said Pablo.
"*¡Qué mágico!* The camera is turning Cusco's
barking into singing!" Dora said. "So that's why you
ran away, Cusco? We'll help you find *tus hermanos.*
¡Vamos, perrito!"

Sniffing out his brothers' scent, Cusco followed his nose to the park, where Dora saw her friend Emma.

"Am I glad to see you!" Emma said to Dora. "I was sitting on the bench, practicing my violin, when I saw a puppy chase a squirrel up that tree. Now he's stuck!"

"Aww, poor little guy. He's too scared to come down," Dora said.

"I know just the song to help calm him," said Emma.

"*Tranquilo, perrito,*" she sang softly.

"Let's sing with Emma," Dora said. "*Tranquilo, perrito.*"

Listening to the song, the puppy calmed down and jumped into Pablo's arms.

Everyone was happy to
see Cusco and his brother
back together—even Pablo.

But the celebration was cut short when Dora's friend
Kate came running toward them. She was dressed in
a dog costume, and a little puppy ran behind her.
Running behind them both was a gang of alley cats!
Dora turned her camera on, and the cats' loud
meows changed to singing.

"*We're alley cats, and we move real fast.*
Chasing dogs always makes us laugh!"

"Help! I was on my way to perform in a puppy play for Doggie Adoption Day when I found this puppy," Kate cried. "And then these alley cats started chasing us! How do we get them to stop?"

"Cats hate to get wet," Pablo pointed out. "Too bad it's not raining."

"My magic charm bracelet
can help with that," Dora said.

"To get a rain cloud to appear, we have to say *¡Nube mágica!*"
As soon as the words were spoken, a cloud grew from the
charm, and it began to rain. The alley cats ran away!

"Nice work, Dora," said Kate. "Come on! We'd better hurry to Doggie Adoption Day."

"But we've only found two of Cusco's brothers," said Dora. "We still need to find his third brother. *¡Mira!* It looks like Cusco has already picked up his scent!"

Cusco's powerful nose led them all the way to an ancient pyramid, where their friend Naiya greeted them.

"*Hola, Naiya.* Cusco's brother went down into the pyramid," said Pablo. "We need to save him."

"*Esperen, amigos,*" Naiya warned. "I know this pyramid, and it's full of booby traps!"

"Map App can help us guide the puppy out," said Dora. "Say 'Map App!'"

"Map App!" Dora's friends cheered.

"Oooh," said Map App. "I can show you the paths inside the pyramid. Then you can tell the puppy which way to go to avoid the booby traps and get out!"

"*¡Perrito!*" Dora called down to the puppy. "First you
need to go right on the sun path."

"Then go left on the moon path," Naiya added.

"And then go right again on the star path," called Pablo.

Following their directions, Cusco's brother made it
out of the pyramid safe and sound!

Cusco was very happy to be reunited with all of his
brothers. Dora pointed her camera at him as he sang:

"We found my three brothers—hip, hip, hooray!
Now we can find homes at Doggie Adoption Day!"

Just then, Dora's phone beeped and Alana appeared on the screen.

"Dora! Doggie Adoption Day is about to start, but I don't know if enough people will show up to adopt all these doggies!"

"*Tengo una idea,*" Dora said. "If we email our video of Cusco and his brothers to everyone we know, then lots of families will come to adopt the doggies!"

Dora and her friends sent the video to all their friends and their families.

"I hope this works!" Emma said.

By the time Dora and her friends got to the animal
shelter, the line for Doggie Adoption Day was around the
block! Everyone worked together to make it a big success.
Kate performed her puppy play while Emma played her
violin. Naiya handed out doggie bones to all the families
adopting new pets.

"I'm so happy all the doggies found homes!" said Dora.
"And we adopted puppies for our homes, too!" Kate said.
"Even Pablo," Dora said. "He adopted Cusco!"
Cusco wagged his tail and licked Pablo's face.
"Awww," said Dora. "I guess Pablo is a dog person after all."

Get to Know Dora and Her Friends!
With Dora, Every Day Is an Adventure!

Dora may have moved to Playa Verde, but she's still an explorer! She leads her new group of best friends on adventures in the big city, where they work together to make a difference. She's a great student, singer, musician, and athlete, but most of all, she's a great best friend!

Pablo Is Always Up for Adventure!

Pablo never turns down an opportunity to explore new places with his pal Dora. He's funny, friendly, and curious. He loves playing sports, inventing things, and making his friends laugh.

Emma Rocks!

Emma is an amazing musician who can play guitar, violin, and piano. She's so good that she helps out the younger musicians in the elementary school band. She may seem shy, but when she's onstage with an instrument, she really shines!

Kate Takes the Stage!

Kate loves the spotlight and the sound of applause. She's a born storyteller who not only writes plays, but also performs them for her friends. She loves reading stories and trading books with Dora.

Alana Scores!

Alana is great at sports, especially soccer. She's one of the most popular girls at school . . . and one of the nicest. She loves animals and volunteers at the local shelter.

Naiya Is a Star!

Naiya is one of the smartest girls in Dora's school. She loves math and science, and you can often find her gazing at the stars through her telescope or studying animals in nature. Plus, she speaks three languages!

In Playa Verde,
magical adventures await
Dora and her friends at
every turn!